Dear Parent:

Congratulations! Your child is taking the first steps on an exciting journey. The destination? Independent reading!

STEP INTO READING® will help your child get there. The program offers five steps to reading success. Each step includes fun stories and colorful art. There are also Step into Reading Sticker Books, Step into Reading Math Readers, Step into Reading Write-In Readers, Step into Reading Phonics Readers, and Step into Reading Phonics First Steps! Boxed Sets—a complete literacy program with something for every child.

Learning to Read, Step by Step!

Ready to Read **Preschool–Kindergarten**
• big type and easy words • rhyme and rhythm • picture clues
For children who know the alphabet and are eager to begin reading.

Reading with Help **Preschool–Grade 1**
• basic vocabulary • short sentences • simple stories
For children who recognize familiar words and sound out new words with help.

Reading on Your Own **Grades 1–3**
• engaging characters • easy-to-follow plots • popular topics
For children who are ready to read on their own.

Reading Paragraphs **Grades 2–3**
• challenging vocabulary • short paragraphs • exciting stories
For newly independent readers who read simple sentences with confidence.

Ready for Chapters **Grades 2–4**
• chapters • longer paragraphs • full-color art
For children who want to take the plunge into chapter books but still like colorful pictures.

STEP INTO READING® is designed to give every child a successful reading experience. The grade levels are only guides. Children can progress through the steps at their own speed, developing confidence in their reading, no matter what their grade.

Remember, a lifetime love of reading starts with a single step!

www.seussville.com   www.catinthehat.com   www.stepintoreading.com

Educators and librarians, for a variety of teaching tools, visit us at www.randomhouse.com/teachers

Library of Congress Cataloging-in-Publication Data
Worth, Bonnie.
Cooking with the cat / by Bonnie Worth ; illustrated by Christopher Moroney. — 1st Random House ed.
    p.   cm. — (Step into reading. A step 1 book)
"Based on the motion picture screenplay by Alec Berg & David Mandel & Jeff Schaffer."
SUMMARY: The Cat in the Hat bakes cupcakes in this simple retelling of a scene from the movie version of Dr. Seuss's classic book.
ISBN 0-375-82494-4 (trade) — ISBN 0-375-92494-9 (lib. bdg.)
[1. Cookery—Fiction. 2. Cats—Fiction. 3. Stories in rhyme.]
I. Moroney, Christopher, ill. II. Title. III. Series: Step into reading. Step 1 book.
PZ8.3.W896 Co 2003   [E]—dc21   2003007281

Printed in the United States of America   First Edition   40 39 38 37 36 35 34 33

STEP INTO READING®

STEP 1

COOKING
with the
CAT

By Bonnie Worth
Illustrated by Christopher Moroney

Based on the motion picture screenplay by
Alec Berg & David Mandel & Jeff Schaffer

Based on the book by Dr. Seuss

Random House 🏠 New York

Look! Look!
The Cat wants
to cook!

Look! A book!
The Cat has
a cookbook!

COOKING
WITH THE
CAT

By the Cat
in the Hat

We need
a tin!

Which tin
will win?

The thin tin
is best.
Put back
the rest.

11

We need
ham and jam.

Lots and lots
of pots.

We spot
the pot!

Hot shot

into the pot.

A pot shot!
(Not so hot!)

We take
a seat.
We start
to beat.

No, no, no!
We do not eat
the treat
we beat.

Do not
slop
the glop
on top.

Stop! Stop!

Stop that glop!

Mop up
that glop!

Do not
drop
the mop
in glop!

We heat
the treat.

A spot

on the pot!

Got the pot!

Ding!

They are done.

A neat seat
to eat a treat!

We eat
and eat
and eat
and eat!

This treat

cannot

be beat!